THE
WOULD-BE
WITCH

RUTH CHEW

THE WOULD-BE WITCH

with illustrations by the author

A STEPPING STONE BOOK™

Random House New York

To Buck

Visit us on the Web!
randomhousekids.com
SteppingStonesBooks.com

Educators and librarians, for a variety of teaching tools, visit us at
RHTeachersLibrarians.com

Library of Congress Cataloging-in-Publication Data
Chew, Ruth, author, illustrator.
The would-be witch / by Ruth Chew ; with illustrations by the author. —
First Random House edition.
p. cm.
"A Stepping Stone book."
Summary: When a small white cat follows them home from Zelda's antique store,
Robin and Andy find themselves in the middle of an adventure involving magic
polish that brings anything it touches to life, and a coven of would-be witches.
ISBN 978-0-449-81567-0 (trade) — ISBN 978-0-449-81570-0 (tr. pbk.) —
ISBN 978-0-449-81569-4 (ebook)
1. Witches—Juvenile fiction. 2. Magic—Juvenile fiction. 3. Brothers and sisters—
Juvenile fiction. [1. Witches—Fiction. 2. Magic—Fiction.
3. Brothers and sisters—Fiction.] I. Title.
PZ7.C429Wo 2014 813.54—dc23 2013035053

Printed in the United States of America
10 9 8 7 6 5 4 3 2 1
First Random House Edition

This book has been officially leveled by using the F&P Text Level Gradient™
Leveling System.

THE
WOULD-BE
WITCH

"Rob, look at the poor little cat! She's shut up all by herself." Andy Gates pressed his nose against the window of the shop.

His sister Robin watched the fluffy little white cat pick her way among a set of old dishes that had purple violets painted on them. The cat sidestepped a little china lady and squeezed between a huge plaster frog and a tall thing that looked like a fountain.

The little cat stood on her hind legs and tried to crawl up the plate glass. She opened her pink mouth to meow. But Robin and Andy couldn't hear her through the window.

Robin moved her finger back and

forth across the glass. The cat tried to catch Robin's finger.

"You're lonely, and you want to play," Robin said.

"I don't remember this store. Wasn't this where the delicatessen used to be?" Andy looked up at the sign across the top of the plate glass window:

ZELDA'S AT HOME

In the window there was a smaller sign:

Come in and Browse

Andy tried the door. It was locked. "How can we go in and browse? Zelda isn't home."

A very small sign in the corner of the window said:

We buy and sell

Robin peeked through the glass door.

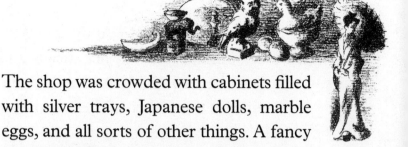

The shop was crowded with cabinets filled with silver trays, Japanese dolls, marble eggs, and all sorts of other things. A fancy old clock with a swinging pendulum stood against the wall.

Robin remembered that their mother had asked her to buy a loaf of rye bread. The bakery was in the next block. "Come on, Andy." Robin took a last look at the little white cat. The cat looked back at her with round blue eyes. Suddenly the cat caught sight of something. She gave a jump and knocked over a glass vase.

A shadow fell across the window.

Robin and Andy turned around. They saw a little old woman dressed all in black. She was fishing a large key out of her handbag. The old woman fitted the key into the lock and opened the door of the little shop.

"She must be Zelda," Andy said.

The woman turned her head and looked at the two children. She had the greenest eyes that either of them had ever seen.

Through the open door of the shop they could hear the old clock striking five. Robin grabbed Andy's hand. She pulled him after her down Church Avenue toward the bakery.

"What's the hurry for, Rob? I want to look at the things in Zelda's." Andy's legs were shorter than Robin's. He had to run to keep up with her.

"It's Friday," Robin reminded him. "The bakery closes early."

When they reached the bakery, the man behind the counter was already putting the cakes away. There were only three loaves of bread left on the shelf. Robin bought the last loaf of rye bread.

On their way out of the store Andy

nearly tripped over a small white cat. He bent down to pet it. "Hey, Rob, doesn't this look like the cat in Zelda's?"

Robin looked at the cat. "Yes," she said. "Maybe it ran out when Zelda opened her door."

"Let's take it back to her." Andy bent down to pick up the cat. It dodged him and ran under a parked car.

"It's getting dark, and Mother's waiting for us." Robin took hold of her brother's hand and started for home. When they came to the old house where they lived, Robin and Andy walked up the stone steps to the front door. Andy rang the doorbell.

Mrs. Gates opened the door. Something streaked between Robin's legs and ran into the house.

It was the white cat.

2

The cat ran up the stairs in the front hall. Andy tore after her.

"What's that?" Mrs. Gates looked up the stairway.

Robin handed her mother the paper bag with the loaf of bread in it. "It's Zelda's cat."

"Who is Zelda?" Mrs. Gates asked. She opened the paper bag and sniffed the rye bread.

"She's the lady who has the funny little store where the delicatessen used to be," Robin said. She stuck her nose into the paper bag.

Andy came downstairs. He was carrying the cat. "Let's keep her, Mom. She followed Rob and me home. She doesn't want to stay with Zelda."

Mrs. Gates looked at the fluffy little cat. "Don't be silly, Andy. You'll have to take her back. But it's suppertime now. You and Robin can take the cat home after supper. Go and wash your hands. Your dad is hungry."

"I'll put the cat in my room for now." Andy went back upstairs with the cat.

Robin followed her mother into the kitchen. Mr. Gates was standing in front of the stove. He lifted the lid on a saucepan and peeked inside. Robin ran to give her father a hug. "What's for supper, Daddy?"

"Franks and beans," Mr. Gates told her.

"My favorite," Robin said. She went to get the silverware to set the table.

After supper Andy cleared the table and then went to his room. Robin put the dirty dishes into the dishwasher. When she had finished she went upstairs. The door of Andy's room was closed. Robin tapped on the door.

The door opened a crack. Andy looked out. When he saw Robin, he said, "I found this cat chasing my marbles all over the room. She gets into everything."

Robin walked into Andy's bedroom. It looked as if a bomb had hit it. There were schoolbooks scattered across the floor. The spread had been yanked off the bed, and the pillow had a small hole in one end.

The feathers were leaking out. Andy was on his hands and knees, picking up the marbles.

The white cat was chasing a feather across the top of Andy's desk. When she saw Robin, the cat sat down and looked at her with round blue eyes. The feather was sticking out of one side of the cat's mouth.

Robin laughed. "You're a mischief, little cat," she said, "but I wish we could keep you for our own. Would you like that?"

The cat stood up and jumped off the desk. She ran over to Robin and rubbed against her leg. Robin picked up the fluffy little cat and held her against her cheek. "You must be hungry, and I don't have anything to feed you. I'll have to take you back to Zelda right away."

Mrs. Gates was standing in the doorway. "It's raining," she said. "And I really don't want you children out after dark. Tomorrow's Saturday. You can take the cat back to Zelda right after breakfast. Bring her down to the kitchen now. I'll give her a bowl of milk."

The little cat purred loudly.

Robin wanted the cat to sleep in her room. Andy insisted she ought to spend the night in his. Mrs. Gates settled the argument. She took an old baby blanket out of the linen closet and put it in a cardboard box under the kitchen table. The cat turned round and round in the box until she made just the right kind of dent in the blanket. Then she curled up and went to sleep. Robin thought the cat looked like a round powder puff in the box.

Next morning, when Robin came down to breakfast, she found the cat licking the last scrap from a tuna fish can.

"I'm going to make a tuna casserole for supper," Mrs. Gates explained. "The cat is cleaning the can."

"Oh, Mother, do we have to take her back to Zelda?" Robin opened a box of cornflakes.

Her mother handed her a container of milk. "I wish we could keep her, Robin. And I'd ask Zelda if she would sell her cat, but right now we can't afford anything extra."

Andy came into the kitchen. "Zelda buys and sells stuff, Mom. She's got all sorts of junk in that store. Maybe she'd trade the cat for something."

Mrs. Gates looked at Andy. "Go comb your hair. And are you sure you brushed your teeth?"

Andy went back upstairs. Mrs. Gates went to the breakfront in the dining room. She looked through the glass door at the crowded shelves. "Most of these things I never use. The silver things are tarnished." She opened the breakfront and took out a pair of silver salt and pepper shakers. They were shaped like birds. Mrs. Gates took them into the kitchen and put them on the table.

"I bought a jar of silver polish just last week from an old man who came to the door. I didn't really want the polish, but I was sorry for the old man." Mrs. Gates took a small jar out of her sink cabinet. She put it on the table beside the silver birds. "Now we'll see how well this stuff works."

The telephone on the kitchen wall rang. Mrs. Gates answered it. "Hello," she said. "Yes, yes. I'll be there as soon as I can." She hung up the phone. "That was my boss. He wants me to work today.

I have to rush. Make the beds for me, please, Robin. And get Andy to help you clean up the breakfast dishes." Mrs. Gates ran upstairs to change her dress.

Robin picked up the salt shaker. Andy came back into the kitchen. "What have you got there?" He took the pepper shaker off the table.

Andy looked at the silver bird in his hand. "Maybe we could trade these to Zelda for her cat."

Robin looked at the salt and pepper shakers. "They're almost black." She unscrewed the cap on the jar of polish and dipped her finger into the pink creamy stuff inside. She rubbed a little on the head of the silver bird.

Where Robin put the polish a tiny spot of silver gleamed through the black tarnish. Robin didn't rub any more on the salt shaker, but the spot began to get bigger. It grew and grew until the salt shaker shone all over.

Suddenly the cold metal felt different in Robin's hand. It was warm and feathery. Then it moved!

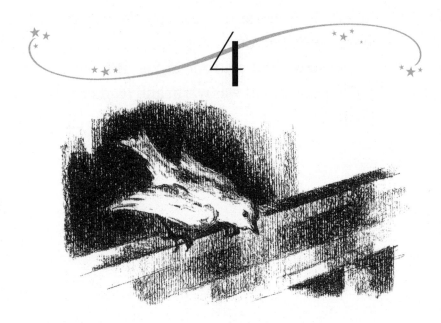

4

Robin was holding a live bird in her hand. Its feathers shone like silver. The bird cocked its head and looked at Robin with bright dark eyes.

"Meow!" The cat jumped onto the kitchen table.

The little bird fluttered out of Robin's hand and flew onto the molding over the door. Andy looked up at it. Then he stuck his thumb into the jar and smeared polish on the head of the other silver bird. An instant later Andy was trying to stop the pepper shaker from flying away. "Grab the cat, Rob!"

The cat dodged Robin and knocked the toaster off the table. Robin caught the toaster before it hit the floor. "Careful!" she said to the cat. The cat looked ashamed and sat down in the middle of the table.

Mr. Gates walked into the room. "What's all the noise about? Get off the table, Cat. You don't belong there."

The cat jumped off the table. She upset the container of milk. Robin ran to get a rag to mop up the mess.

Andy kept the little bird hidden in his hands. He walked into the dining room and put the bird on a shelf of the break-front. He closed the breakfront door and went back into the kitchen.

Mr. Gates poured himself a cup of

coffee from the pot on the kitchen stove. "Weren't you supposed to take that cat back to the antiques store?"

"We will, Daddy," Robin said, "just as soon as we've made the beds and cleaned up the kitchen." She was hoping her father wouldn't notice the bird perched over the door.

Mr. Gates dropped a slice of bread into the toaster. He took a jar of marmalade out of the kitchen cabinet. The little bird sat very still.

Robin started putting dirty dishes into the dishwasher. "Andy," Robin said, "take the cat upstairs. And start making the beds. I'll come up in a minute to help you."

Andy grabbed the cat and went out of the room.

Mr. Gates saw the jar of pink polish on the table. He picked it up and read the label aloud. "New Magic Polish. Does wonders with silver, china, glass, wood, rubber, and plastic."

While Mr. Gates was busy reading, the little bird fluttered down and perched on Robin's shoulder. Robin walked into the dining room and opened the door of the breakfront. The bird hopped in and sat down on the shelf beside the other one. They looked just like a pair of silver salt and pepper shakers.

Robin wasn't sure if they needed air. Just in case they did, she left the door of the breakfront open a crack. Then she went back into the kitchen to finish loading the dishwasher.

5

Robin and Andy were on their way to Zelda's. Andy carried the cat. "I wonder if Zelda would trade the cat for a pair of live silver birds."

"I want to keep them," Robin said. "There must be something else we could trade for the cat."

They turned the corner onto Church Avenue. It was a dark wintry day. The lights were on in Zelda's little store. A bell jangled when Robin opened the door. The two children walked into the store.

Zelda was busy with a customer. A fat lady in a pink hat was holding a blue and white teapot. "This is exactly what I want," she said. The lady put the teapot on the counter and opened her handbag.

Zelda looked up and saw the children with the cat. "You've brought back my Pearl! I thought she was gone for good." She reached for the cat.

Pearl jumped out of Andy's arms. She landed on the counter and kicked the china teapot onto the floor. It smashed into a dozen pieces. The lady gave a little scream.

Zelda frowned. "It's all right," she said to the lady. "I can get another one just like it. Can you come back in about an hour?"

"That will be too late," the lady said. "I'm giving a tea party this afternoon. I'm afraid I'll have to go somewhere else for a teapot." She turned and walked out of the store.

"I'm sorry, Mrs.—" Andy said.

"Oh, it's not your fault. Pearl is the clumsiest cat in the world. And you'd better call me Zelda. Everyone else does." The little old woman bent over to pick up the pieces of the broken teapot. Robin got down on her hands and knees to help her.

23

Zelda took a brass tray out of one of the cabinets in the store. Robin put all the pieces of the teapot on the tray. The old woman put the tray on a shelf in the back of the store. She walked around, humming to herself as she straightened the things on the countertop.

Zelda picked up an old oil lamp with a glass chimney and polished it with a piece of Kleenex. Then she put the lamp away in a cabinet. "I can't have Pearl knocking *that* over," she told Robin. She stroked a little wooden turtle under the chin. "You'd better go in the window today. You might like to see what's going on in the street."

Andy was looking at a big glass alligator. "Isn't this great, Rob? I wish I had it for my room."

Robin wasn't sure she liked the alligator. She preferred the little china skunk or the hound dog with the tail that moved up and down when she touched it. Everywhere Robin turned in the shop she saw interesting things.

The little white cat was crouching beside the cash register. Her eyes were shut, but the end of her fluffy tail twitched. She didn't look happy.

"Zelda," Robin said. "I like Pearl a lot. Would you trade her for something?"

"No," the old woman said. "One thing I really must have is a cat. If you want to visit Pearl you might come in and mind the store for me this afternoon. I have to be out between four and five o'clock."

Robin thought for a minute.

"Meow!" Pearl jumped down from her perch by the cash register and ran to rub against Robin's leg.

"I'll come," Robin said.

Andy was listening. "What about me?"

Zelda looked at him hard. "Just don't sell anything to anybody. Find out what they want, and tell them I'll be back later. Good-bye now. I'll expect both of you at four o'clock."

The two children ran all the way home. Their father was in the living room watching a football game on television. Robin and Andy went into the dining room. The door of the breakfront was open about two inches. The little silver birds were gone.

"What will Mother say?" Robin said.

"What would she say if she saw the live birds?" Andy answered. "It's better this way."

Robin went into the kitchen. The silver birds were sitting on the table. The one who had been a salt shaker looked up and gave a hungry little cheep.

Robin remembered that her mother kept a big bag of birdseed in the basement laundry room. She used it to fill the bird feeder in the back yard. Robin found a pie pan in one of the drawers of the sink cabinet. Then she went down the back stairs to get some seed.

When she came back to the kitchen Andy had filled the sink with water. The silver birds were splashing in it.

Robin put the pan of birdseed in the middle of the kitchen table. "Here, Salt. Here, Pepper," she called.

Salt hopped onto the sink top and shook himself like a puppy dog. Then he flew to the table to peck at the birdseed. Pepper took time to smooth her feathers with her beak before she joined the other bird. Both birds dropped the shells from the seed all over the table and the floor.

Andy watched them. "They're a messy pair," he said. "We'll have to sweep the room when they're finished."

Robin expected the birds to go back into the breakfront when they were done with their meal. Instead they flew up into the air and winged their way through the house to the front hall. Then they flew upstairs.

"What do you suppose they're up to?" Robin said.

Andy ran up the stairs after the birds. Robin followed him. She found her brother in the upstairs hall. He was moving his head round and round as he watched the birds fly from room to room. "They keep going back to your room, Rob."

Robin went into her bedroom. She had left the door of her closet open. The birds flew into the closet. Robin's Easter basket was in the corner of the high shelf in the closet. There was still some purple Easter grass left from last year in the basket.

Salt and Pepper were excited. They flew around picking bits of fluff off the blankets.

"What do they want that stuff for?" Robin asked.

"Take a look in the closet, Rob," Andy said. "Those crazy birds are building a nest in your Easter basket."

During the early part of the afternoon Robin and Andy were busy cleaning up the kitchen after the birds. Robin took the pan of birdseed up to her room and set it on the shelf in her closet. She put an old raggedy wool sweater on her bed. The wool was just what Salt and Pepper wanted for their nest. They flew onto the bed and began to try to unravel the sweater. Robin sneaked out of the room and closed the door.

It was just four o'clock when the children got back to Zelda's. The old woman was waiting for them at the door. "I was afraid you weren't coming," she said.

"Meow." The fluffy little cat came running to the door.

Zelda leaned over and grabbed the cat. "Pearl always tries to sneak out whenever the door is opened." She handed the cat to Andy. "Hang onto her."

The old woman went to the back of the store. She took a long black cloak down from a peg and put it on. Then she stood on a chair to get a large hatbox off a high shelf. She opened the box and looked into it. "I hope you like my new hat." She took out a wide-brimmed hat with a tall pointed crown.

When Zelda put on the hat Andy said, "You look just like a witch in that get-up."

Zelda giggled. "Do I? Well, I must hurry. Now remember, don't sell anything. I'll be back at five o'clock." She walked to the door. Before she opened it she turned and pointed her long bony finger at the cat. "Now, you, Pearl, behave yourself!"

When the old woman was gone, Robin took off her jacket. She fished something out of the pocket and then went to hang up the jacket. She walked over to the shelf at the back of the store where Zelda had put the tray with the pieces of broken teapot.

Andy hung up his jacket. He turned and saw what Robin had in her hand. "Rob, what are you going to do? That's the magic polish!"

"I thought it might mend the teapot Pearl broke," Robin said. "The label says it works wonders with china."

Andy ran to look at the bits of china on the brass tray. "Rob, look! It's already mended!"

Robin went to see. A blue and white teapot was on the tray.

"She did a neat job," Andy said. "You can't see the cracks."

Robin stared at the teapot. It looked as if it had never been broken.

"You know what I think, Rob." Andy lowered his voice to a whisper. "I think Zelda is a *witch.*"

"Maybe," Robin said. She looked at the floor. It was thick with dust. "She's messy enough to be one," she said. "I wonder where Zelda keeps her broom." She put the jar of polish on the tray beside the teapot and began to look for the broom.

The cat Pearl followed Robin wherever she went in the store. Once Robin almost stepped on her. Robin looked in all the corners and behind the counter. At last she saw the broom. It was wedged between one of the cabinets and the wall. Robin reached behind the cabinet to get it. The cat jumped onto her shoulder. "Stop it, Pearl!"

Pearl rubbed against Robin's neck and licked her ear with her rough pink tongue.

The bell over the door jangled. The fat lady in the pink hat walked into the store. "I can't find a decent teapot anywhere," she said. "Where's Zelda?"

Andy picked up the blue and white teapot. "Zelda's gone out. She'll be back at five o'clock."

The lady walked over to Andy. Before he could stop her she took the teapot out of his hands and handed him a five-dollar bill. "Give this to Zelda."

"Zelda said we mustn't sell anything while she's out," Andy said.

"I don't have time to argue. The guests

for my tea party will be arriving any minute." The lady started for the door.

Robin ran after her. The cat was still on her shoulder. "Please, don't take the teapot. Zelda will be angry with us!"

"Just be sure you give her the money," the lady in the pink hat said. She opened the door and went out.

Robin went back to get the broom. "I can't reach it."

Andy grabbed the corner of the cabinet. "Help me pull this away from the wall."

Together the children moved the heavy cabinet. Andy squeezed behind it to get the broom. Something small and furry ran between his legs and raced across the dusty floor. It was a mouse which had been hiding behind the cabinet.

The cat jumped off Robin's shoulder and ran after the mouse. Round and round the little store they went. Pearl knocked over a silver candlestick and spilled a dish of seashells. She upset a vase of fake flowers.

The mouse ran up the chains of the old clock. Pearl tried to follow her. Robin grabbed the clock and held it steady. Then she picked up the fluffy little cat and put her on a high stool in the corner. "Leave the mouse alone, Pearl."

The cat sat down and began to clean herself.

"I wonder why Zelda won't give Pearl to us," Robin said. "She's a terrible cat to have in a store like this."

Robin collected the fake flowers and stuck them in the vase. She put the sea-shells back into their dish.

The broom was very old and raggedy. "It doesn't look much good," Andy said. "Zelda ought to get a new one." He started to sweep the floor.

A cloud of dust began to rise. Andy coughed and sneezed.

Robin opened the shop door to get a little air. "This is awful," she said. "I read a story once about a broom that swept by itself." Robin had an idea. She put her hand over her nose and mouth and ran through the cloud of dust to where she had left the magic polish on the brass tray. "Bring the broom here, Andy."

Robin unscrewed the lid and dipped her fingers into the jar. She smeared a little pink polish onto the broom handle.

"Sweep!" Robin said to the broom. The broom began to sweep the floor.

"Get your jacket, Andy." Robin took hers down from the peg and put it on. "We can wait outside until the dust clears."

Robin and Andy had to dodge the busy broom as they went to the door of the shop. Robin opened the door just wide enough for them to squeeze out. The two children stood outside the store and looked through the glass door to watch the broom work. It swept all around the store and gathered the dust into a pile.

"It needs a dustpan," Robin said. "And Zelda doesn't have one."

"I'll go home and get ours." Andy ran down Church Avenue and turned the corner onto the street where he and Robin lived. Robin went on watching the broom. It was still sweeping. The dust was piled in a mound in the center of the floor. Robin remembered the rest of the story about the broom that swept by itself. The boy who used it couldn't stop it sweeping.

Robin wondered if she would have the same trouble.

When Andy came back with the dustpan the children took it into the store. The broom at once swept dust into the pan. When it was full Robin took the pan outside to dump the dust into the gutter. Then she brought it back for another load. After she had made three trips with the dustpan there was still dust in a pile on the floor.

"Rob," Andy said, "you're doing it the hard way." He opened the jar of magic polish and smeared a little on the dustpan. "Do your job, Pan," Andy said.

The dustpan gave a little shake. It flew over to the pile of dust. The broom swept a load onto it. Andy held the door open, and the pan sailed out to dump the dust into the gutter.

A lady with a baby carriage was walking down the sidewalk. She ducked when the dustpan came flying out the door of the little antiques store. The lady put the brake on her carriage and walked into the store. She was angry. "Who threw that dustpan? It nearly hit my baby."

Just then the empty dustpan swooped back into the store. Robin grabbed it. "Rest for a minute," she whispered to the dustpan. It stayed still in her hands.

The lady turned to see who had thrown the dustpan back into the store. While her back was turned, Andy grabbed the broom. The broom jiggled, but Andy held onto it.

The lady glared at the children. "Be careful what you're doing." She went out of the store and pushed her carriage away down the sidewalk.

Andy wrapped his legs around the broom. It flew about a foot up from the floor and took a turn around the shop.

Robin watched it. "That broom seems to be better at flying than sweeping."

"Of course, Rob," Andy said. "That must be what Zelda uses it for."

"Meow!" The fluffy little white cat was still sitting on the high stool in the corner of the store.

Robin put down the dustpan and went to pick up the cat. "No wonder you don't like it here, Pearl. You're not at all the type to be a witch's cat."

"Talking of witches," Andy said, "Zelda ought to be here pretty soon." He jumped off the broom. "Back to your corner, Broom!"

The broom dropped to the floor and slowly shuffled to its place behind the cabinet.

"I'm glad this broom does what it's told," Robin said.

It was nearly five o'clock. Robin set Pearl on the floor and helped Andy shove the cabinet closer to the wall. Then she put the jar of magic polish into her jacket pocket.

Robin began to wonder what the witch would do when she found they'd sold the teapot. She looked around the little store at the china lady and the plaster frog, the glass alligator, and the hound dog. Maybe they were once alive! Was Pearl afraid Zelda would turn her into a china cat? Robin could just imagine Andy made of wood like the turtle. Suddenly the back of her neck felt prickly. And she was cold all over. Robin shivered.

The bell over the door jangled. Zelda walked into the store. "Did I have any customers?" she asked the children.

Robin looked up into the old woman's green eyes. She took a deep breath. "Only one," she said. "The lady in the pink hat came back for the teapot."

Andy handed Zelda the five-dollar bill. "She gave me this to pay for it."

Zelda took the money.

Robin wanted to run out of the store before the witch could do anything to her. But she was too frightened to move.

Andy picked up the dustpan. "We cleaned up the store a bit."

Zelda looked at what was left of the pile of dust in the middle of her floor. "Thank you," she said. "That was kind of you."

She was still wearing the long cape

and the funny pointed hat. There was a round mirror with a curly frame on the wall beside the old clock. Zelda went to look at herself in it. She sighed and took off her hat.

Andy walked to the door. "Good-bye, Zelda."

"Good-bye." Robin turned to look at the witch. Zelda was still holding her hat. Slowly the old woman took off her cape and went to put the hat away in its box.

Robin and Andy left the store. They walked to the corner. When they turned onto their own street Robin started to run. Andy chased after her. They didn't stop running until they came to their own house.

Robin rushed up the front steps and rang the bell. She had to ring three times before her father answered it.

The football game on television was still going on.

"Robin, have you seen that jar of silver polish I had this morning?" Mrs. Gates was looking into the breakfront in the dining room. "Now what could I have done with the salt and pepper shakers?"

Robin went to get the magic polish out of her jacket pocket. She handed it to her mother.

Mr. Gates turned off the television set in the living room and walked into the dining room. He laughed when he saw the jar of polish. "Read the label on that stuff. It claims to clean everything from wood to plastic."

Mrs. Gates looked at the label in silence. Then she opened the jar. "Robin, this stuff is half gone! And the label says, 'Keep out of the reach of children'!" Mrs. Gates put the jar in her apron pocket. "I hope you and Andy didn't eat this."

Andy was in the kitchen. He came into the dining room. "Of course not, Mom. We took it to Zelda's to work on some of the things in her store."

Mrs. Gates looked at the bread and peanut butter in Andy's hand. "You'll spoil your supper," she said.

Robin ran upstairs before her mother could ask her any more questions. She wanted to see what the birds were doing.

The door to her bedroom was still closed. Robin opened it just wide enough to slip through. Then she closed it behind her. She turned on the light. She didn't see the birds.

Robin looked in the closet. The pan on the shelf was empty. The shells from the birdseed were scattered on the floor of the closet.

Then Robin saw Salt. He was perched on the end of her clothes pole near the wall. His head was tucked under his silvery wing.

Robin went to get her desk chair. She put it in the closet and stood on it to peek into the Easter basket. In the basket was a nest. It was woven of the yarn from her old sweater together with the purple Easter grass, a tassel pulled from Robin's bedspread, two hair ribbons, and some ice cream pop sticks Robin was saving. The birds had lined the nest with blanket fluff. Pepper was sitting on the nest. She opened a sleepy eye and looked at Robin.

Robin heard her bedroom door open. She jumped down from the chair.

"It's only me, Rob." Andy shut the door. He walked over to the closet. "Mom says she's locking up the magic polish so we won't get into it." Andy saw the chair. "Did you get a look at the nest?"

Robin nodded.

Andy climbed up on the chair. He had to stand on tiptoe to see into the Easter basket. When he saw Pepper, Andy reached up and lifted the little bird out of the nest.

"Oh," Robin said. "Don't!"

Salt took his head out from under his wing. When he saw what Andy was doing he flew off the clothes pole and pecked at him.

Andy stretched as tall as he could and looked over the rim of the Easter basket. He whistled.

"What is it?" Robin asked.

"See for yourself." Andy moved over on the chair. Robin climbed up beside him and looked into the nest.

Side by side were two little silver eggs.

Andy put Pepper back on the nest. She settled down over the eggs. Salt flew back to his perch on the clothes pole. Robin took the chair out of the closet and closed the closet door.

The two children went downstairs for supper.

Robin was quiet during most of the meal. When it was time for dessert, she said, "Mother, is there really such a thing as a witch?"

Mrs. Gates smiled. "Nowadays, there's

a fad for witchcraft. People like to call themselves witches. They join clubs and have secret meetings and claim to have magic powers. It's all pretty silly."

"Can they do magic?" Andy asked.

"Not really," his mother said.

Mr. Gates put down his spoon. "Magic is like everything else. If you believe it, it's true for you. Not for anybody else, just for you."

Mrs. Gates was thinking. She finished her Jello. Then she said, "Some people make *other* people believe that they can do magic things."

"But what about flying brooms?" Andy persisted.

His mother laughed. "I've never seen one," she said. She looked at Andy's empty dish. "How about some more Jello?"

After the dishes were in the dishwasher, Robin took the dustpan and a whisk broom to her room. She wanted to sweep up the shells from the birdseed. Andy joined her. He opened the closet door and peeked in.

Salt was still perched on the clothes pole. He raised his head and looked at Andy. There was a nervous twitter from Pepper in the Easter basket.

Robin looked at the birdseed shells on the closet floor. "Help me clean up this mess."

"You don't need two people for that job," Andy told her. "Just sweep the shells into a pile, and the dustpan will be there, ready for loading."

He was right. As soon as Robin needed it, the dustpan slid across to her. "I wish we could put some polish on this whisk broom," Robin said.

When all the shells were loaded onto the pan Andy opened the window. "Dump that stuff in the garden," he said.

The dustpan flew out of the window

and scattered the birdseed shells between the rose bushes in the Gateses' back yard. Then the dustpan flew back up to Robin's window. It sailed into the house and landed neatly on the rag rug beside Robin's bed.

Robin closed the window.

Andy looked at the dustpan. His mother had bought it long ago. It was made of hard rubber. Once it had been bright blue, but the color had faded with time. There was a small chip gone from one corner, yet the dustpan was still sturdy.

Andy sat down on it. The dustpan wasn't big enough for him to be comfortable. Still he thought he could stay on it if

he held tight to the sides. "Fly, Dustpan!"

The dustpan rocked under Andy, but it couldn't get off the floor.

"You're too heavy for it, Andy," Robin said. "Dustpan, don't strain yourself."

At once the dustpan was still.

Andy stood up. Robin started to close the closet door. The children heard a little twittering noise.

"Wait a minute, Rob. I'd better check the nest. Maybe Pepper laid another egg." Andy put Robin's desk chair in the closet and climbed up on it. He reached up to lift Pepper off the nest.

Salt flew at Andy and pecked his hand.

"Ow!" Andy took his hand off Pepper and swung at Salt. Salt dodged and flew back onto the clothes pole.

Robin pulled her brother off the chair and out of the closet. "Stop bothering the birds, Andy." She put the chair back in front of her desk and went to close the closet door. Something shiny caught Robin's eye.

Two little silver feathers were lying on the floor of the closet. Robin picked them up. "Aren't they beautiful, Andy?"

Andy's hand was still sore from the peck Salt had given him. He grabbed the feathers. "Beautiful yourself!" He stuck a silver feather behind Robin's ear.

Suddenly Andy couldn't see Robin anywhere.

12

"Rob," Andy called. "Where are you?"

A very small voice answered. "I'm right here. But what's happened to you?" The voice sounded like Robin's. It seemed to come from the floor. Andy looked down.

A little person no bigger than the silver

birds stood beside the dustpan. Andy got down on his hands and knees to get a better look. "Rob!"

"Don't get so close to me when you talk, Andy. I'm afraid you'll blow me away," Robin said. "How did you get so big?"

Andy backed away from her. "I'm not big. You're small. If you don't believe me, take a look at the dustpan."

Robin went over to the dustpan. It looked like a small platform with a wall at the back and a ramp in front. The handle reminded Robin of the high tail of a jet airplane.

Robin walked up the ramp and sat down near the back wall. "Dustpan," she said, "please take me for a ride."

The blue dustpan rose slowly up into the air. It circled the room once and then flew back to the floor. Robin gave it a little pat. "Thank you," she said. "That was fun."

Andy got up off his hands and knees. "You have all the luck," he said. "Why can't I be small?"

"Watch where you walk, Andy," Robin said. "I wouldn't be so lucky if you stepped on me."

Robin wanted to see how she looked. She ran to the tall mirror on the closet door. In the mirror she caught sight of the silver feather Andy had stuck behind her ear. The feather had become small too. Robin pulled it out to look at it.

She blinked her eyes. Suddenly everything in the room seemed to have shrunk.

"Hey, Rob," Andy said. "You're back to your own size again."

"So is the feather," Robin said. "Do you still have the other one?"

Andy had forgotten all about the silver

feathers. "No," he said. "I must have dropped it." He looked at his sister. "Do you think it was the feather that made you small?"

Robin nodded. "They're not just ordinary birds, you know." She began to look around the room. At last she saw the other silver feather. One end of it was poking out from under her bed. Robin picked it up.

"Hold still, Andy." She tucked the feather behind her brother's ear.

Instantly Andy was even smaller than Robin had been. He looked up at her. "Wow!" he said. "You're enormous!" He remembered the dustpan. "Now it's my turn." Andy ran toward it.

Before he reached the dustpan, Robin bent over and grabbed him.

Andy struggled. "Put me down, Rob. I want to go for a ride. And I'm not just going to fly around in your bedroom. I want to go somewhere interesting."

Robin held her brother firmly in her fist. "You listen to me, Andy Gates. I want to fly just as much as you do. But I want to do it right."

Robin pulled the feather out from behind Andy's ear.

Crash! Robin dropped Andy onto the floor. He was too big for her to hold.

Andy stood up and rubbed the seat of his pants. "Take it easy, Rob."

Mrs. Gates opened the door of the room. "What was that awful bang?"

"Robin grabbed me, and I fell," Andy said.

"You know I don't allow horseplay in the house. Anyway it's past your bedtime, Andy. Hurry and take your shower. Then Robin can have hers. I want you two out of the bathroom, so I can take a hot bath. This has been a busy day." Mrs. Gates went downstairs.

Andy made a face. "It's all your fault, Rob."

"Go take your shower," Robin said, "or Mother will make you go to bed early tomorrow night."

Andy left the room. Robin hid the two feathers in the bottom drawer of her desk. She peeped into the closet. Salt and Pepper were both asleep in the Easter basket. Robin could just see the top of Pepper's silvery head. Quietly she closed the closet door.

Robin opened her window and looked out. A lopsided moon was high in the sky. There were lights in the windows of the houses and apartment buildings. And Robin could see the glow from the tall streetlights. She looked down. The

magnolia tree in the yard gleamed white in the moonlight. Robin shut the window.

She undressed and put on her robe and slippers. When Andy had finished in the bathroom Robin went to take her shower and brush her teeth.

Mrs. Gates came to kiss her goodnight after Robin had gone to bed. "Sleep well," her mother said.

But Robin couldn't sleep. She lay in bed and thought of all the things that had happened during the day. She heard her father come upstairs and go to bed. At last the house was quiet.

The clock in the hall downstairs struck eleven times. A board creaked outside Robin's door. She sat up in bed.

Andy tiptoed into the room. He was dressed and had on his outdoor jacket. "Rob," he whispered, "don't be such an old stick-in-the-mud. I want to go for a ride on the dustpan."

14

Robin got up and began to dress in the dark. "Andy," she said, "would you get my jacket, please? It's in the hall closet downstairs."

Andy went to get the jacket.

Robin took the silver feathers out of her desk drawer. She put them into the pocket of her jeans.

When Andy came back with her jacket, Robin put it on. She opened the window and found the dustpan in the dark. Robin pulled the two feathers out of her pocket and handed one to Andy. Then she stepped on the dustpan.

Andy tucked the feather behind his ear. At once he was tiny. He wanted to get on the dustpan, but Robin's feet took up all the room. She tucked her feather behind her ear. Now she was small too. Andy joined her on the dustpan.

The children sat with their backs to the wall of the dustpan. They could see out over the ramp. "Fly," Andy said to the dustpan. It rose into the air.

"Out of the window, please," Robin said.

The blue dustpan sailed out into the night. It was much blacker than it had been when Robin looked out of her window earlier in the evening. The moon had sunk behind the rooftops. And most of the windows were dark. The magnolia tree was lost in the shadows. But the tall lamps glowed above the empty streets.

The dustpan hovered over the back yard. It seemed to be waiting for them to tell it where to go. A black cat squeezed through the picket fence and ran to the back of the yard. It climbed over the high board fence and jumped to the ground behind it.

"Dustpan," Andy said, "follow that cat!"

The dustpan swooped over the fence. The cat trotted through the dry leaves and sticks in the vacant lot between the houses. The dustpan flew low and without a sound. It stayed about ten feet in the air above the cat.

At one end of the block there was a garage and a short driveway to the street. The cat climbed to the roof of the garage, ran across it, and jumped to the driveway. The dustpan followed a few feet behind.

When the cat reached the sidewalk, it raced to the corner and streaked down to East Fourth Street. The black cat slowed to a walk. It dodged under parked cars and slunk in the shadows of the trees. It seemed to Robin that the cat didn't want anyone to see where it was going.

The dustpan bobbed up and down as it followed the cat. Robin and Andy lay on their stomachs and looked over the end of the ramp. They held tight to the edge of the pan to keep from sliding off.

An old brick house stood on East Fourth Street near the corner of Church Avenue. It didn't look like an apartment building, but once at least six families

had lived there. Now it was empty. The windows on the two upper floors were broken. Most of the glass was gone. Sheets of metal had been nailed over the basement and first-floor windows. The neighborhood children had painted fancy designs and scrawls on the metal plate that covered the front door.

The black cat ran down the driveway between the old house and the one next to it. It climbed the high fence at the back of the house and jumped into the bare branches of a skinny tree.

The dustpan skimmed along after the cat. It hovered in the air over the tree. Andy and Robin leaned over the edge and watched the cat.

The cat clawed its way up the trunk of the tree until it reached an upper branch. Then it crawled along the branch until it was close to one of the back windows of the second floor of the house.

The cat gave a leap and jumped through the empty window frame into the house. The dustpan flew down to the window and went in after the cat.

The children were in a shadowy room. The only light came through the broken window. Andy thought this was an old kitchen. He could just make out where the sink had been ripped away. There were pipes still poking out of the wall.

The cat trotted through an open doorway into the next room. From there it went to a hallway. There was a stair in the hall. The cat ran down to the floor below. The dustpan floated after it.

It was much darker here. No light could come through the metal plates on the windows. Robin and Andy grabbed each other to be sure they were both still there. Robin's heart began to pound.

The cat's feet made no sound, but they kicked up a cloud of dust. The children covered their mouths and noses to keep from choking.

At last they saw a dim light. It came from another flight of stairs. The black cat ran down, and the dustpan followed it. The light grew brighter. It glowed red.

15

Robin and Andy were in the basement of the old house. The low ceiling was criss-crossed with pipes and beams. The dustpan hovered near the top of a metal pole which held up one of the big wooden beams.

The red glow came from a fire which burned under a huge iron pot in the middle of the concrete floor. Around the pot was a circle of black cats. Andy counted. There were eleven of them. When the cat the children had been following joined the others, there were twelve.

The brew in the pot bubbled and hissed. Suddenly one of the cats jumped onto the rim of the pot.

Andy and Robin saw the cat dip a paw into the brew. "Meow!" The cat closed its eyes and jumped into the iron pot. The children thought the brew would boil over. It rose to the top of the pot and foamed over the rim. Then the bubbling stopped. A very wet cat climbed out.

"Something's wrong," the cat said.

"You're still a cat, Hester," one of the other cats said.

"So are you." The first cat shook herself. "And so are we all unless we can find out what's the matter."

A scraggly old cat with a tattered ear spoke up. "Can't you count, Hester? There are only twelve of us here. We have to be thirteen or this stupid brew won't work."

"Who is missing?" the first cat asked. She jumped off the rim of the iron pot and walked around the circle of cats. "It's Annabel," she said after she had looked at each set of whiskers. "The greedy thing has been living in the butcher shop. The butcher must have put a bell on her."

A scrawny little cat stepped forward. "I'm sorry I ever chose to be a witch," she said. "If I'm stuck being a cat all the time it isn't worth it. I'd rather go back to that job wrapping packages."

Andy was leaning so far over the edge of the dustpan that he slipped and fell. He landed on the furry back of one of the black cats.

"Yeow!" She shook herself. Andy tumbled to the floor.

He looked up into fierce yellow eyes. Andy knew just how a mouse must feel about cats. He started to run.

"Pull out the feather!" Robin screamed.

Andy reached up and yanked the silver feather from behind his ear.

The cats drew back and stared at the boy. They all sat down in front of him. The yellow eyes seemed to flicker like little lights. Andy wasn't sure what he could do if all twelve cats decided to jump at him. He moved back until he was against the pole. He was afraid to turn his back to the cats.

The cats began to move forward. Inch

by inch they were getting closer to Andy. All at once he made a dash and rushed straight into the crowd of cats. For a moment they were too surprised to do anything. Andy raced up the stairs.

He ran down the dark hall and up to the very top of the house.

The cats were right behind him now. Andy leaned out of a window. Something bumped against his hand.

It was the dustpan.

Andy grabbed the front of it. He put the feather behind his ear. At once he was so small that he was dangling in the air, holding onto the ramp of the dustpan.

Robin pulled him up onto the platform. "Home, Dusty!" she said.

"Dusty flew up the stairs and out of a second-floor window," Robin told Andy. "Then he flew up to the top floor where you were. It was all his own idea."

Before she went to bed Robin made Andy give her the magic feather. She locked it up in her desk with the other one.

In the morning she went down to the laundry room and filled her pockets with birdseed. She put the seed in the pan on her closet shelf. Pepper stayed on the nest. Salt kept flying to her with his beak full of seed.

Andy came into the room and looked at the birds. He put Robin's desk chair in the closet and climbed up on it. Salt made a flying dive at Andy's head.

Robin shook the chair. "Get down, Andy." She pulled him off the chair and out of the closet. Then she put the chair back in front of her desk and closed the closet door.

Mr. Gates made French toast for breakfast. Mrs. Gates was reading the Sunday paper at the kitchen table. Robin was just finishing her second piece of toast when she heard a yowl from the back yard.

Mr. Gates looked out of the kitchen window. "It's a cat fight!"

Andy opened the back door. A black cat was chasing a white one across the fence. The white cat took a flying leap off the fence. It bounded across the yard and through the open door into the kitchen.

"Pearl!" Robin said.

The little cat ran to her and rubbed against her ankle. Robin picked her up.

She could feel the cat's heart thumping
under the fluffy fur.

Mrs. Gates reached over to pet the cat.
Pearl looked up at her and purred.

"Oh, I wish we could keep you," Mrs.
Gates told the cat. "But you belong to
Zelda. Robin, you'd better take her back
to the store right after breakfast."

"It's Sunday," Robin reminded her mother. "The store is closed."

"Maybe Zelda is there anyway," Mrs. Gates said. "You'd better go and see. If we feed Pearl, she'll keep coming back here."

How could Robin explain to her mother that Zelda was a witch? Robin was almost sure that the black cat that was chasing Pearl was Zelda. Zelda may even have been one of the witches in the old house last night. She had turned into a cat and couldn't turn back.

Robin had to go alone to return the cat. Mr. Gates insisted that Andy stay home and help him put up a shelf over his workbench.

Some of the Church Avenue stores were open on Sunday. People were going in and out of the candy store on the corner. And the man in the dairy store was selling milk and eggs. But Zelda's at Home was closed.

Robin pressed her nose against the glass door and looked into the shop. Someone was sitting in the back reading a book. It was Zelda!

17

Robin tapped on the door of the shop. Zelda was wearing glasses to read. She looked over the top of the glasses to see who was knocking. Then she put down the book and came to open the door.

"Oh, it's you, Robin. And you've

brought back my Pearl again! She slips out of the store whenever I open the door. And she seems to like you better than me." The old woman looked at the fluffy little cat. She blinked her eyes as if to keep from crying. Her long pointed chin quivered.

Suddenly Robin felt sorry for the witch. She touched the little old woman's wrinkled hand. "What's the matter, Zelda?"

"I'm not sure. Maybe it's just that I'm not clever enough." Zelda tried to smile. "Well, come in for a few minutes, dear." She opened the door wide.

Robin stepped into the store. "You were reading," Robin said. "I love to read." She went over to the counter where Zelda had put the book and picked it up. *The ABCs of Magic.*

"Just something I found in the library," Zelda said.

"But why would you want a book like this?" Robin asked. "You are a witch."

"Not really," Zelda said in a sad little voice.

"You look like a witch to me," Robin insisted.

"Do I, dear?" Zelda's green eyes began to twinkle behind her glasses. "I'm only a would-be witch. If I could join the coven, I'd be a real one."

"What's a coven?" Robin asked.

"It's a kind of witches' club," Zelda explained. "I failed the entrance exam for the third time yesterday. I don't think they'll let me take it again."

"Oh, Zelda," Robin said, "you don't need to join that nasty gang of cats. You're a great witch already."

"What do you mean?" Zelda asked.

"You mended the teapot so it was just like new," Robin reminded her.

"It *was* new," Zelda said. "I bought it

from a wholesaler on Thirteenth Avenue yesterday afternoon. You and Andy were the ones who did the magic. You sold it for twice what I paid." She sat down in a chair and hid her face in her hands.

Robin touched Zelda's bony shoulder. It was shaking. "But how about your broom?"

Zelda looked up. Her lined old face was streaked with tears. "Broom?" she said. "What broom?"

Robin pointed behind the cabinet. "This one."

Zelda stood up and walked over to see where Robin was pointing. "Oh, that thing. It isn't even any good to sweep with. I ought to get a new one."

Robin looked at the broom. It was just the magic polish that had enchanted it after all.

"Zelda," she said, "can you reach the broom?"

Zelda's arms were much longer than Robin's. She pulled the broom out from behind the cabinet.

"Now," Robin said, "put it between your legs."

Zelda grinned. "Wait a minute." She took her long black cape down from the peg and swirled it around herself. Then she got down her hatbox from a shelf. She lifted out the wide-brimmed, pointed hat and put it on. Zelda straddled the broom. She turned to look at herself in the round mirror beside the clock. "Pretty good for a would-be witch," she said.

"Now, hold tight," Robin told the old woman, "and tell the broom to fly."

Zelda took a good grip on the broom and got ready to jump into the air. "Please, Magic Broom," she said, "take me for a ride."

The skinny little woman didn't weigh much. The broom rose up into the air with

no trouble at all. It looped twice around the shop. Zelda was so surprised that her hat fell off her head and she kicked over the vase of fake flowers.

"You need practice," Robin yelled. "Watch your head and keep your ankles together!"

Zelda's gray hair came loose from the bun at the back of her head. It streamed out behind her. "Whee!" she said.

"Those crazy birds chased me out of my own bedroom," Robin told Andy. "I opened the closet and they both flew at my face. I had to run out of the room and shut the door. If Mother goes in there it'll be awful."

"Put a sign on your door, DANGER, BIRDS!" Andy suggested.

Robin and Andy were in Andy's room at the end of the hall. They left the door open so they could see if anybody went to Robin's room.

"The dustpan and the magic feathers are in there," Robin said. "We'll need them tonight."

"Why?" Andy asked. Robin had told him about her visit to Zelda. "Are we going flying beside your silly would-be witch? She didn't know her old broom was magic. You could have asked her to give it to us. I know I'd be good at broom riding."

"We've got the dustpan, Andy. Don't be greedy." Robin saw her father walk over to her bedroom door. "I'm in Andy's room," she called to him.

Mr. Gates came down the hall. "I want to take your mother to a movie," he said. "I told her you're old enough to fix your own supper. There's some tuna fish casserole left in the refrigerator. And you can open a can of peas."

"What about dessert?" Andy asked.

"I hadn't thought about dessert," his father said.

"I know how to make tapioca pudding, Daddy," Robin told him. "Don't worry about anything. You and Mother have a good time."

"When will you be home?" Andy wanted to know.

"Not till very late," Mr. Gates said. He walked back down the hall.

Robin went downstairs to the kitchen. Her mother was looking in the refrigerator. "I told Dad I'd make tapioca pudding," Robin said. "Why don't you go and get dressed to go out?"

Mrs. Gates gave Robin a hug and ran up to her room to change.

"Everybody always thinks you're such an angel," Andy said. "I wonder what

they'd say if they knew you were big bud-
dies with a witch."

Robin opened the cabinet and took
down a box of tapioca. "Andy," she said,
"while you're over by the refrigerator,
could you get out an egg?"

Robin stacked the tapioca bowls in the dishwasher. "I told Zelda where the witches meet. She never even knew they turned into cats. She's been trying to get a black cat for years, but none of them wanted to have anything to do with her."

Andy laughed. "Of course not. They're *real* witches. Zelda's just a make-believe. Where did she take her witchcraft tests?"

"In one of the empty classrooms on the third floor of our school," Robin said. "Now she's going to that basement to talk to the witches. I don't trust those awful cats, Andy. I'm afraid they'll do something to her."

"You forget," Andy said, "they need a thirteenth witch."

"I want to go and watch what happens at the witches' meeting," Robin said. "But first we have to get Dusty and the magic feathers out of my room. Salt and Pepper won't let anybody in there."

"No problem," Andy said. "Remember that television show about beekeeping? Birds aren't as bad as bees."

Robin shook her head. "Oh, no, you don't, Andy Gates! The beekeepers *smoked* the bees out of their hive. You know Mother and Daddy don't want us playing with fire."

"There you go with the angel act again," Andy said. "Who said anything about smoke? I was thinking of the nets the bee people had over their heads."

Robin turned off the kitchen light. She and Andy went upstairs. Andy pulled the bedspread off his bed. He wrapped it around himself. Even his head was covered. He left only a little place to see out.

"This ought to protect me from those birds," Andy said. He opened the door of Robin's room.

Salt and Pepper flew out and winged their way down the hall.

"Put the bedspread away, Andy," Robin said. "And go get your jacket." She went into her room.

Robin unlocked her desk drawer and took out the silver feathers. She found the dustpan where she had left it in the corner of the room.

"What about the birds? They'll be flying all over the house," Andy said.

"We can't waste time trying to catch them now. They're probably just looking for more food." Robin took the pan off the closet shelf and ran down to the laundry room to fill it with seed.

Then she put on her jacket and zipped it up. "Come on, Andy."

"What's the hurry?" Andy asked.

"I want to get to that old basement before the witches so we can hide and watch them," Robin said.

"Does Zelda know we're going to be there?" Andy wanted to know.

"No. She thinks only her broom is magic." Robin opened her bedroom window. She stepped onto the dustpan and handed Andy one of the silver feathers. Then she tucked the other feather behind her ear. At once she was small. Robin sat down and held tight to one wall of the dustpan.

Andy still held his feather in his hand. "Why do we have to go back into that dark hole, Rob? We were lucky to get out of it last night."

"You don't have to come if you're afraid," Robin said.

Andy stuck the silver feather behind his ear.

20

The fire under the giant pot of witches' brew was almost out. By the dim red glow Andy and Robin saw one black cat curled up on the concrete floor near the pot. She seemed to be asleep.

The blue dustpan flew back to its hiding place by the metal pole. Robin and Andy lay on their stomachs to look down over the ramp. They both held tight to the edge.

One by one, without a sound, the black cats came down the stairs into the basement. Robin silently counted. At last she whispered to Andy, "That makes twelve."

A cat stood up and stretched. She looked like the cat who had jumped into the brew last night. "Edna!" the cat hissed. "You're asleep on the job again. I've a good mind to expel you from the coven."

The cat who was asleep woke up. "Did I hear right? Expel me? I wish you would, Hester. I'm tired of this witch business."

Hester cleared her throat. She pretended not to hear. "Witches," she ordered, "go and get fuel for the fire."

The cats went back up the stairs. Edna started to curl up again near the pot. Hester gave her a slap. "You too," she said. "And be careful how you talk to me!"

Edna's ears flattened. She slunk off

after the other cats. Hester lay down to
wait for their return.

Robin and Andy were watching. Suddenly Hester jumped to her feet. She
arched her back. All her fur stood on end.
And her tail became as fat as a squirrel's.

Hester's yellow eyes gleamed. They
were reflecting the light from a little lamp
with a glass chimney that seemed to be
floating down the stairs into the dark basement.

The cat moved back into the shadows.

As the lamp came closer, Robin and
Andy saw that someone was holding it,
someone in a pointed hat who was riding
a broom. "It's that crazy Zelda," Andy

whispered. "Why would she bring an oil lamp?"

Zelda flew round and round the basement, shining her lamp into all the dark corners. At last she caught sight of the end of Hester's tail. It was sticking out from behind an old pail. "Here, kitty, kitty," Zelda called.

At the sound of Zelda's crackled old voice the black cat's ears pricked up. She crawled out into the open and looked up at the old woman.

"Zelda!" the cat said.

Zelda craned her neck to look down at the cat. "You know me, pussy cat?"

"Of course. I gave you the witchcraft exam three times." Hester arched her back and stretched her claws. Her fur began to flatten, and her tail went back to its usual size.

Zelda was staring down at the cat. "You must be Hester Blackstone," she said. "Please, won't you give me another chance. I do so want to be a witch."

"You've never passed the test," the cat told her, "but that broomstick trick ought to qualify you. When the other witches come back with fuel for the fire I'll talk to them about it."

"Oh, thank you. Thank you." Zelda was so excited that she almost fell off the broom.

The black cat watched her with narrowed eyes. "I have to talk to the others in private," she said. "Go up to the top floor of this house and wait until I send for you."

The old woman gave the broom handle a little pat. "Up we go, Buster," she said. The tattered broom flicked its straws and flew up the stairway.

21

The black cat watched until Zelda had disappeared from sight up the stairway. She began to pace back and forth. In a little while the other cats returned. One cat carried the broken rung from a chair in her mouth. Another balanced a small wooden crate on her back. Four of the cats struggled under the weight of a little sled. Some cats brought cardboard boxes. Others had newspapers. They all stuffed their loads under the big iron pot. The flames grew higher, and the dark brew started to steam.

The dustpan hovered up near the wooden crossbeam. Robin and Andy lay on their stomachs and watched the cats. They hardly dared to breathe.

"What's the use of heating up the brew when there are only twelve of us?" the scraggly old cat asked. "We're just wasting fuel and knocking ourselves out for nothing."

Hester jumped up onto the rim of the pot. "Witches, listen!" she said. "I have found a thirteenth."

The cats all turned to her.

"Most of you know Zelda," Hester said.

"Oh, *no!*" a chorus of cats wailed.

The scraggly old cat strutted over to the pot. "Hester," she said, "you must be out of your mind. Zelda just isn't the type. You know she's taken the standard true and false test several times. And she always makes a mess of it. That woman even keeps a *white* cat who breaks things. And then she says the cat can't help being clumsy! Find somebody else for the thirteenth witch. Zelda would ruin the coven."

Hester had been standing so long on the rim of the pot that her feet were getting hot. She jumped into the crowd of cats. "Listen to me," she hissed in a hoarse whisper. "Zelda has found a real flying broom. And not one of us has ever been able to get hold of one. You know that all we have for magic is this watered-down brew. And it doesn't work when it's cold. *I want that broom!*"

The cats gathered close around her. "How are you going to get it, Hester?" a skinny little cat asked.

Hester stroked her whiskers. She winked. Then in a low voice she said, "Simple. We'll all go into the magic brew and turn back into ourselves. Then I'll tell Zelda *she* has to jump into the brew to become a real witch. You know what will happen."

"Zelda will turn into a cat," Edna said. "But if she jumps back into the brew she'll become herself again."

"She'll never get the chance," Hester said. "I'll take the broom *and* the cat."

This struck all the cats as being very funny. They laughed until they rolled on the floor.

The brew was boiling now. "Where's Zelda?" the old cat asked. "We don't want the brew to boil away. You know you lost the recipe for it, Hester. We won't be able to make more."

Hester glared at her. She cleared her throat. "Zelda is on the top floor of this house waiting to be called," she said. "Edna, you go and get her. And be quick about it." She gave the cat a swat with her paw.

Edna bounded up the stairs.

22

Robin and Andy watched Zelda come flying down into the basement. The old woman was very excited. She curled her ankles around the broomstick and held onto it with one hand. In her other hand she was still carrying the oil lamp. Zelda's green eyes were shining. She flew in a little circle over the heads of the cats.

"Zelda," Hester said, "watch what we do. Then you'll know how to become a witch." The cat leaped up onto the rim of the pot and dived into the bubbling depths of the brew. A minute later a woman splashed up out of the pot. She had yellow hair and long red fingernails.

"She looked better as a cat," Andy whispered to Robin.

The scraggly old cat was next. She jumped up on the rim of the pot and tested the brew with one paw before she jumped in.

"Hurry up," Edna said.

The old cat jumped into the brew. She held both paws over her nose and went under. The next minute up bobbed a scraggly old woman. Hester had to help her climb out of the pot. "Pew! That stuff tastes terrible, Hester. Somebody's feet must have been dirty last time we used it."

Hester frowned at her. "Next!" she

said. One by one the cats dived into the pot of brew. And each one turned into a woman.

Now it was Zelda's turn. She was flying round and round right over the steaming pot. "Are you sure I won't be scalded?"

"Of course, Zelda," Hester said. "Didn't you see the rest of us jump into the brew? Now bring your broom over here and put down that lamp. I'll help you climb into the pot."

"Don't do it, Zelda," Robin screamed. Her voice sounded very small.

Zelda turned her head. She thought she'd heard someone call her name, but she wasn't sure.

The witches too had heard something. They looked into all the dark corners of the basement.

"Come on, Zelda," Hester said. "The brew is just hot enough. If you don't jump

in now, it may not work. Don't you want
to be a real witch?"

Zelda looked down into the pot. "Oh,
all right."

"Stop her, Dusty," Robin said.

The dustpan dived down from its
hiding place. It flew right at the little old
woman on the broomstick.

"Come away, Zelda," Robin screamed.

Hester climbed onto the rim of the
pot. She reached up and grabbed hold of
the dustpan.

23

The dustpan tried to fly out of the witch's grasp, but Hester was too strong for it. She stared down at Robin and Andy.

Robin jumped off the dustpan and pulled the silver feather out from behind her ear. She almost fell into the pot of brew, but she landed on the floor beside it. Hester climbed down from the rim of the pot. Robin was back to her own size now. She tried to take the dustpan away from the witch.

Andy jumped onto Hester's shoulder and slipped the feather out from behind his ear. At once he became so heavy that the witch was knocked to the ground.

Andy grabbed the witch's hands. He tried to pull them off the dustpan. Hester held onto it. The boy and the witch rolled over and over on the concrete floor of the basement.

"Somebody get the broom!" Hester yelled.

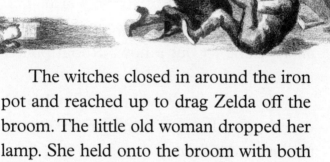

The witches closed in around the iron pot and reached up to drag Zelda off the broom. The little old woman dropped her lamp. She held onto the broom with both hands and zoomed up toward the ceiling.

The oil from the lamp splashed down into the pot. It spread like a lake across the surface of the brew. A moment later the whole pot was a raging fire.

Robin was trying to help Andy take the dustpan away from the witch. "Help me," Hester screamed.

Two witches ran to her aid.

The children never saw the white cat come bounding down the stairs. Pearl leaped on Hester and bit her hand. She let go of the dustpan. Andy grabbed it. He jumped to his feet and ran toward the stairs.

Edna took hold of Robin's arm. The white cat sank her sharp teeth into Edna's ankle. Edna let out a howl. Robin pulled free and ran after Andy.

The blazing brew in the pot boiled over the rim. It ran in flaming rivers across the basement floor.

Zelda swooped down and grabbed the white cat. "Come on, Pearl. We'd better find Robin and Andy."

The would-be witch looked all over the basement. She couldn't see the children anywhere. Zelda flew up the stairs. "Robin! Andy!" she called.

When she reached the first floor something circled around her head. It was the dustpan.

"We're going home, Zelda," Robin yelled at the top of her voice.

The little old woman waved her hand. "A very good idea." She steered her broom up to the floor above and out one of the broken windows.

Robin and Andy heard the pack of witches running up the stairs. The children moved back against the wall at the back of the dustpan. They held tight to the sides. The dustpan soared up to the third floor and out into the cold night air.

24

Mr. and Mrs. Gates were still out when Robin and Andy flew into Robin's bedroom. The children took the feathers out from behind their ears. Robin locked them in her desk drawer. She closed her bedroom window and put the dustpan away in the broom closet downstairs.

Andy remembered Salt and Pepper. He went to look for them. Although he searched all over the house, Andy couldn't find the birds.

"We have school tomorrow," Robin reminded Andy. "And it's late. If Mother and Dad find us up when they come home, we'll be punished."

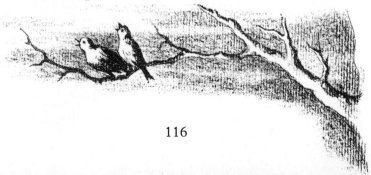

Just then they heard the sound of a key in the front door. Robin and Andy rushed upstairs to bed. Andy finished undressing under the covers.

In the morning when Mrs. Gates came to wake Robin, she said, "What a beautiful day! Spring must be on the way at last." She walked to the window. "Robin, look at those two birds! Aren't they lovely?"

Robin jumped out of bed and ran to the window. Salt and Pepper were sitting in the magnolia tree singing for joy.

Mrs. Gates went to wake Andy. Robin opened her window so the birds could return to their nest. But they didn't seem to want to come back into the house. When Robin went down to breakfast she left her window open and closed her bedroom door.

Mr. Gates was sitting at the kitchen table reading the morning newspaper. "There was a fire in the neighborhood last night," he said. "That old wreck of a house on East Fourth Street burned down. Twelve women were trapped on the top floor."

"How awful!" Mrs. Gates said. She put a bowl of oatmeal in front of Andy.

"The firemen rescued all the women." Mr. Gates folded up the paper. "But now they're in trouble. No one knows who they are. They had no right to be in that house. The owner is going to press charges against them. They may even end up in jail."

Mrs. Gates looked at the clock. "My boss gave me the day off," she said, "but it's time for you to leave for work, John. And the children will have to run to get to school on time." Mrs. Gates poured herself a second cup of coffee. She picked up the newspaper and sat down to read.

25

At three o'clock Robin and Andy walked home from school together. Their mother opened the front door for them. They could tell that she had been housecleaning. She was wearing an apron, and her sleeves were rolled up.

"What a mess your room was, Robin!" she said. "I found the salt and pepper shakers I've been looking for in your Easter basket. What were they doing there?"

"Where are they now?" Robin asked.

"In the breakfront where they belong," her mother told her.

The children went into the house. Andy ran to the breakfront. He stared at the two little silver birds on the shelf. "Rob, come here."

Mrs. Gates had gone into the kitchen. Robin put her school books on the dining room table and walked over to the breakfront.

"Those aren't Salt and Pepper!" Andy whispered.

Robin looked hard at the salt and pepper shakers. "They must have hatched out of the silver eggs," she said. "Salt and Pepper flew out of the window."

Mrs. Gates looked out of the kitchen. "You did a good job of shining the salt and pepper shakers," she said. "They look brand new. But I don't like having silver polish that I have to lock away from you children. This morning I walked past Zelda's at Home. No wonder you children took the polish there. Everything in her window needed cleaning. So I gave Zelda the jar of polish." Mrs. Gates smiled. "And you'll never guess what happened! Come into the kitchen, children. I have a surprise for you."

Robin and Andy turned away from the breakfront and walked into the kitchen. There, on the floor, just finishing a bowl of cat chow, was Pearl.

Mrs. Gates stooped to stroke the fluffy little white cat behind the ears. "Zelda said we could have her. But she warned me that Pearl breaks things."

"Meow." Pearl arched her back and purred.

"What's the matter, Robin?" her mother asked. "Aren't you happy to get the cat?"

"Of course, Mother," Robin said. "I'll

go and thank Zelda." She ran to the front door.

Andy picked up the cat and followed his sister. "Why the hurry, Rob?"

Robin yanked open the door. "I have to stop Zelda before she polishes that glass alligator!"

Let the magic continue. . . .

Here's a peek
at another bewitching tale
by Ruth Chew.

THE
WITCH
AT THE
WINDOW

"Hey, Marge, look at this!" Nick bent down to pick up something that had fallen out of a fat old beech tree.

Marjorie saw that her brother was holding a long-handled wooden spoon. She stared up into the branches overhead. "Hello!" she called. "Is anybody up there?"

There was no answer.

Nick handed Marjorie the spoon. "Maybe somebody left it in the tree."

Marjorie felt the smooth wood. "The wind must have blown it down."

"It's such a big spoon," Nick said. "We could dig with it at the beach."

"Mother doesn't like us to take things that don't belong to us," Marjorie reminded him.

"But if we leave the spoon here in the park," Nick said, "somebody else will pick it up. Then the person who owns it will never get it back."

Marjorie thought for a minute. "We can keep it safe in case we find out who lost it." She tucked the big spoon under her arm.

"I'm getting hungry," Nick said.

Marjorie looked at the blue sky. "I wonder what time it is."

"We'd better not be late for supper again." Nick began to walk along the narrow path that went through the woods on Lookout Mountain.

The two children had spent the afternoon in Prospect Park. Now they went around the big hill until they came to the road that went through the park. Marjorie took a look at the traffic. "It must be rush hour."

While they waited for the light to turn

green, Nick and Marjorie heard a clear, high whistle.

Nick looked around. "What was that, Marge?"

"It's that bird, there. Come on. The light's changing." Marjorie walked quickly across the road.

Nick ran after her. "Marge," he said, "the bird followed us." He pointed to the lowest branch of a chestnut tree.

Marjorie laughed. "What makes you think it's the same bird, Nick?"

"It looks exactly like the one that was whistling at us on the other side of the road," Nick said.

"That's a starling," Marjorie told him. "There are lots of them in Brooklyn. And they all look alike."

The bird was about as big as a robin. It was fat and had a short tail. In the sunlight its black feathers gleamed with purple and green lights.

"It's beautiful!" Nick said.

Marjorie nodded. "I never really looked hard at a starling before." She took a step toward the bird.

The starling flapped up into the branches of the chestnut tree.

"You scared it, Marge," Nick said.

"I only wanted to get a better look," Marjorie told him.

"Well, if all starlings look alike, you'll have another chance." Nick started running toward the park gate.

Marjorie raced after him.

2

Marjorie and Nick lived four long blocks from the park. They ran along Ocean Parkway and turned the corner onto Church Avenue. By the time they reached East Fifth Street both of them were out of breath.

They stopped running and walked halfway down the block.

Nick looked up into the big sycamore tree in front of their house. He grabbed his sister's arm. "Marge, there's that spooky bird! It *is* following us."

"Don't be silly, Nick. I told you there are lots of starlings in Brooklyn." Marjorie climbed the front stoop of the old stone house. Nick came up after her. Marjorie's house key was on a string around her neck. She unlocked the front door.

Their father came into the hall. He hugged both Marjorie and Nick at the same time. "You just made it, kids," Mr. Gordon said. "Any minute now I would have had to set the table. Isn't that your job, Nick?"

Marjorie ran upstairs and hid the big wooden spoon in the bottom drawer of her dresser. Then she washed her hands and went down to the kitchen to help her mother.

At suppertime Marjorie said, "We saw a starling in the park. I never knew they were such pretty birds."

Mrs. Gordon put a carrot stick on

Nick's plate. "In some countries starlings are kept in cages."

"That's awful," Marjorie said. "Birds should be flying around. Why would anybody put one in a cage?"

"Maybe because starlings can be taught to talk," her mother said.

"Like parrots?" Nick asked.

"Don't get any ideas, Nick," Mrs. Gordon said. "I don't like birds in cages any more than Marjorie does."

"Maybe we wouldn't have to keep it in a cage," Nick said. "It could just fly from room to room."

Mrs. Gordon put down her fork. "I'm sorry, Nick. I don't want you bringing any birds into the house. They belong outdoors."

After supper, everybody went into the living room. "*King Kong* is on television tonight," Nick said.

His mother laughed. "You don't want to see that old movie."

"Yes, we do," Nick said.

"It will give you nightmares," Mrs. Gordon said.

"Dad can watch it with us." Nick turned on the television. "He can turn it off if we get scared."

Mrs. Gordon picked up her library book. "I'm warning you. If either of you children wakes up screaming tonight, you'll both go without television for the rest of the week."

Marjorie had never liked scary movies, but she didn't want Nick to know it. He was younger than she was. She sat down on the sofa beside her father.

The movie wasn't nearly as scary as Marjorie had thought it would be. Maybe that was because her friends had told her how it ended.

When the movie was over, Mrs. Gordon closed her book. "Bedtime, Nick."

Nick went upstairs to take a shower and brush his teeth. Then it was Marjorie's turn.

3

"Marge, wake up!"

Marjorie opened her eyes. In the darkness she saw Nick standing beside her bed. "What's the matter?"

"Somebody's outside my window, trying to get in," Nick said.

Marjorie sat up in bed. "Sh-sh! Don't let Mother hear you."

King Kong must have been too scary for Nick after all, Marjorie thought. And if Mrs. Gordon knew Nick had a nightmare, Marjorie wouldn't be allowed to watch her favorite program on Saturday. "I'll go to your room and see what's going on," she told her brother.

Marjorie slipped out of bed and started down the hall. Nick tiptoed after her. His room was at the very end of the hall. As Marjorie came closer to it, she heard a creaky noise.

She reached the doorway. The noise was coming from the window. Marjorie's heart started to pound. A little cold shiver crawled up her back.

She took a deep breath. Then she walked over to the window. Nick came right behind.

Marjorie wasn't tall enough to see over the air conditioner that was in the window. She looked around the shadowy room. "Where's your chair?" she whispered.

Nick went to get his desk chair. Marjorie stepped onto it and lifted one slat of the venetian blind.

Nick climbed up beside her. The two children peeked through the crack in the blind.

They saw two feet in shoes with big buckles on them. The feet were standing on the air conditioner outside. Two thin, bony hands were trying to push up the window Mr. Gordon had taped shut.

Marjorie grabbed the venetian blind cord. She pulled the blind all the way up to the top of the tall window. Now Nick and Marjorie could see that there was a woman on the air conditioner. She was wearing a long dress and a pointed hat with a wide brim.

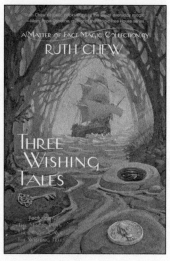